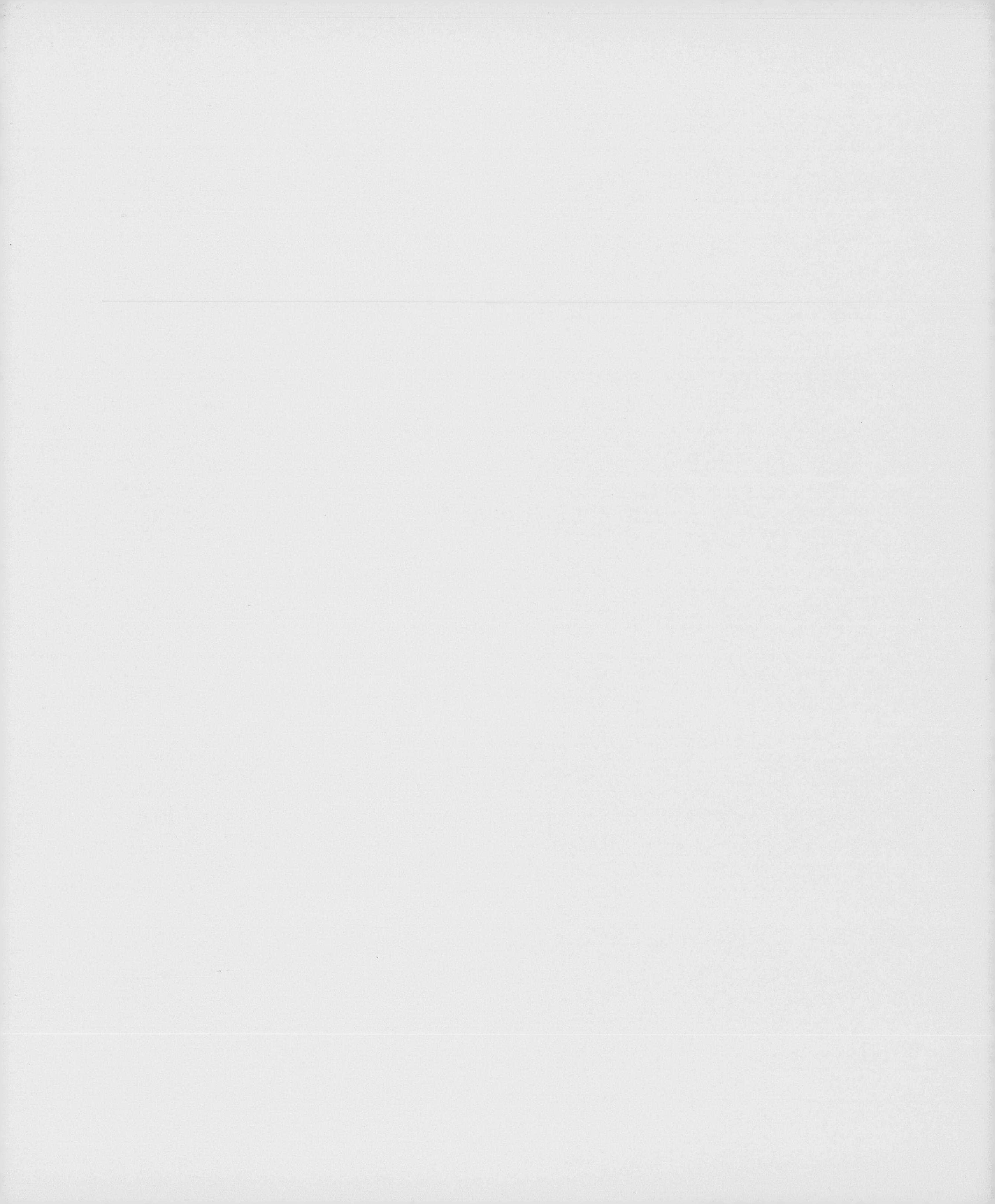

WILDLIFE PARK

For Hera, Fionn, Ruth, Tadhg and
Maia, master storytellers all – S.C.

First American Edition 2020
Kane Miller, A Division of EDC Publishing

First published in Great Britain 2019 by Egmont UK Limited
The Yellow Building, 1 Nicholas Road, London W11 4AN

For information contact:
Kane Miller, A Division of EDC Publishing
P.O. Box 470663
Tulsa, OK 74147-0663
www.kanemiller.com
www.edcpub.com
www.usbornebooksandmore.com

Library of Congress Control Number: 2019942281

Printed and bound in China
1 2 3 4 5 6 7 8 9 10
ISBN: 978-1-68464-045-4

THE
BIGGEST
STORY

SARAH COYLE
DAN TAYLOR

Kane Miller
A DIVISION OF EDC PUBLISHING

Errol's mom told the best stories. They were always fun and exciting. So one afternoon, when there was nothing to do, Errol knew a story was just what he needed.

Unfortunately, there was a plumbing problem.

“Sorry, Errol,” said his mom. “This pipe won’t fix itself. Why don’t **you** think up a story instead?”

Errol blinked, surprised.
Then he shook his head.

"I can't tell a story.

I don't know how."

"Bet you can,"
said his mom.
"Just have a go."

Out in the garden, Errol tried hard to think of a story.

But star jumps didn't shake any ideas out.

And staying upside down for a full minute only made his ears hurt.

He was so busy thinking, he didn't notice the **ants** until . . .

"Psssst!"
said the biggest ant.
"We couldn't help
overhearing that
you're telling a story.
Will it have ants in it?"

"Uh . . .
WOW, sure,"
said Errol.
He'd never met
a talking ant
before. Perhaps
other animals
could talk?

"Ahem . . ."
said a low voice.

A tabby cat was tapping Errol's foot. "You know . . ." she said. "The best stories have **cats** in them."

With an awful kerfuffle, all the neighborhood cats bobbed up onto the fence. Each cat sat at a polite distance from the others. Cats like a bit of space.

"So, what do you say?" asked a tortoiseshell cat.
"Any room for cats in your story?"

Ants and cats! Errol's story was getting better already.

"Hmmm," Errol looked around the garden. "What else does my story need?"

“Stunts!”
shouted a sheep, clipping the gate
as she jumped into the garden.
Showering splinters, a long line
of sheep hopped after her.

“You need **action**!
Excitement!
Paragliding!
Sheep do all that stuff.”

"Done," Errol grinned. He had everything he needed to start his story.

But just then . . .

. . . the ground trembled and shook. A mob of meerkats burst through the fence. Elephants, lizards, pandas, monkeys, even a sleek leopard, followed.

"So . . ." the leopard looked excited. "Word in the wildlife park is you're telling a story. Good news! We're in!"

Errol gave a low whistle. To fit everyone in, this story would have to be big. “Okay,” he said. “But that’s definitely it. There’s no room for anyone else. Not even . . .”

"DINOSAURS!"
shouted the sheep.

A Stegosaurus and a gigantic T. rex stood, beaming, as they sank slowly into the lawn. "A new story is always worth traveling through time and space for," the T. rex explained.

“’Course, we were in the very first stories,”
said the Stegosaurus, smugly.
“Hope this one is as good . . .”

The audience fell silent, waiting for the story to begin. **Errol gulped.** He felt as though he had eaten too much pizza . . . and the pizza was made of bees.

Would his story be any good?

"I've got my tea!" Errol's mom sat down, but didn't seem to notice that her chair was covered in monkeys. "I'm all ready for your story!"

Errol grinned at her. Then he took a deep breath and began . . .

THE BIGGEST STORY

OH NO! T. REX IS IN TROUBLE! SHE'S STUCK IN THE MIDDLE OF...

THOSE TRICKSY CATS HAVE TRAPPED HER!

BUT HERE COME T. REX'S FRIENDS! HOORAY!

POOR T.REX! NOT EVEN HER FRIENDS CAN HELP HER NOW.

WAIT! IS IT? NO, IT CAN'T BE...

IT IS! IT'S THE SUPERHERO SHEEP! GOLDEN GLIDER! SKY ROCKET! SILVER ARROW!

"The End!" said Errol.

Seconds stretched . . .

then the audience went . . .

WILD!

Animals cheered, roared and stomped.

Dinosaurs danced, ants somersaulted,
cats purred louder than lawn mowers and
sheep ping-ponged across the lawn.

Errol's mom pulled him into a huge hug.

"That was the best and the biggest story I've ever heard!" she cried. "Much better than any of mine."

Tired but happy, Errol went upstairs for his bath.
He felt very proud. He had told his own story
and his head was full of ideas for more.

A little later, Errol's boat was sailing past bubble mountains, when he heard a tiny tap-tap-tapping.

A small owl stuck her head through the open window, "Did I miss the story?"

"Yup," said Errol. Crossing the dangerous bathwater deep, the boat began to rock. "But I'll tell you another.

It starts on a **stormy sea** . . ."

Errol had lots of fun making up his story.
If you told a story, what would it be about? After a few star jumps, try out this idea to get started.

Choose a Name

....

....

....

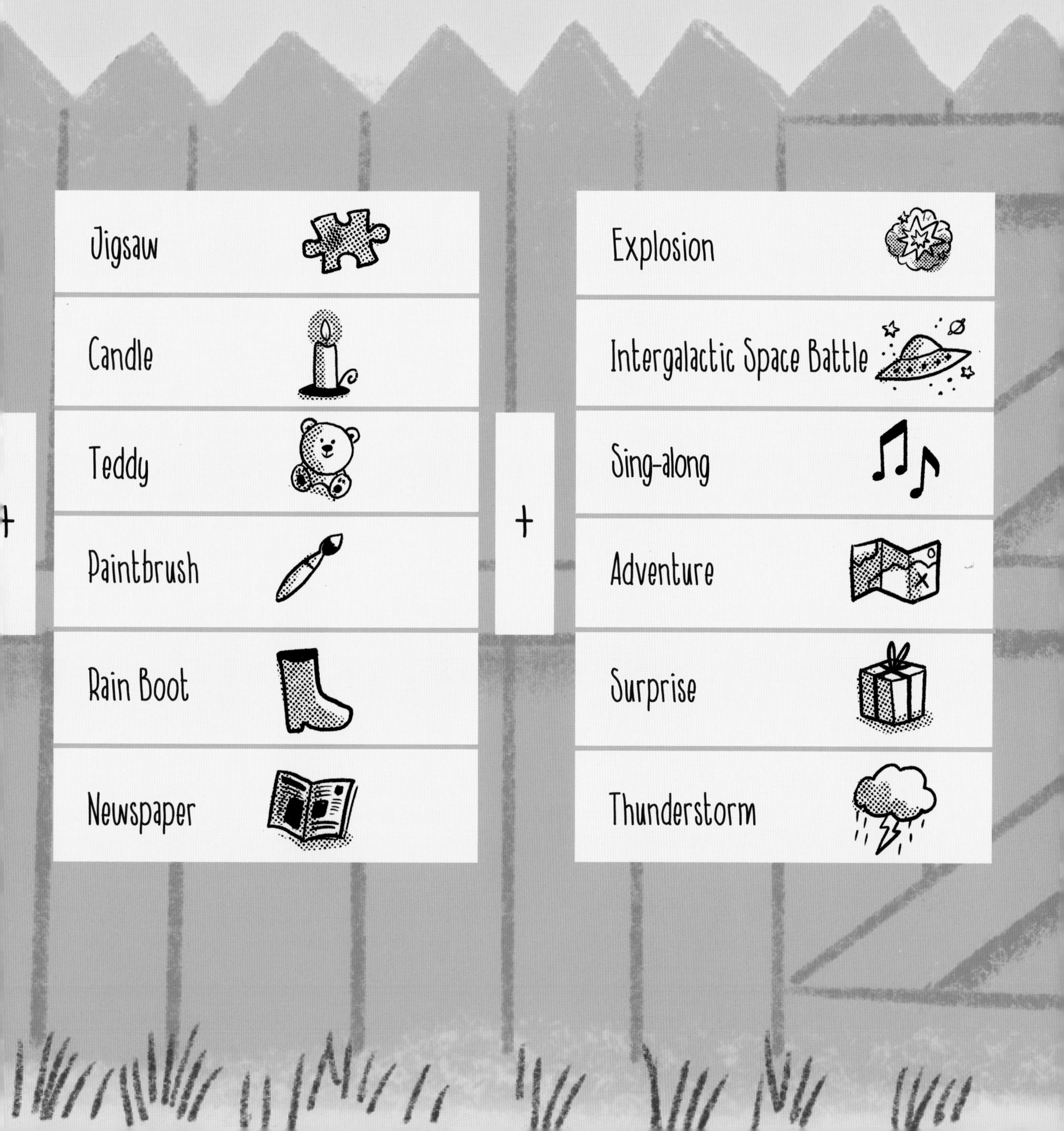
Jigsaw
Candle
Teddy
Paintbrush
Rain Boot
Newspaper
+
Explosion
Intergalactic Space Battle
Sing-along
Adventure
Surprise
Thunderstorm

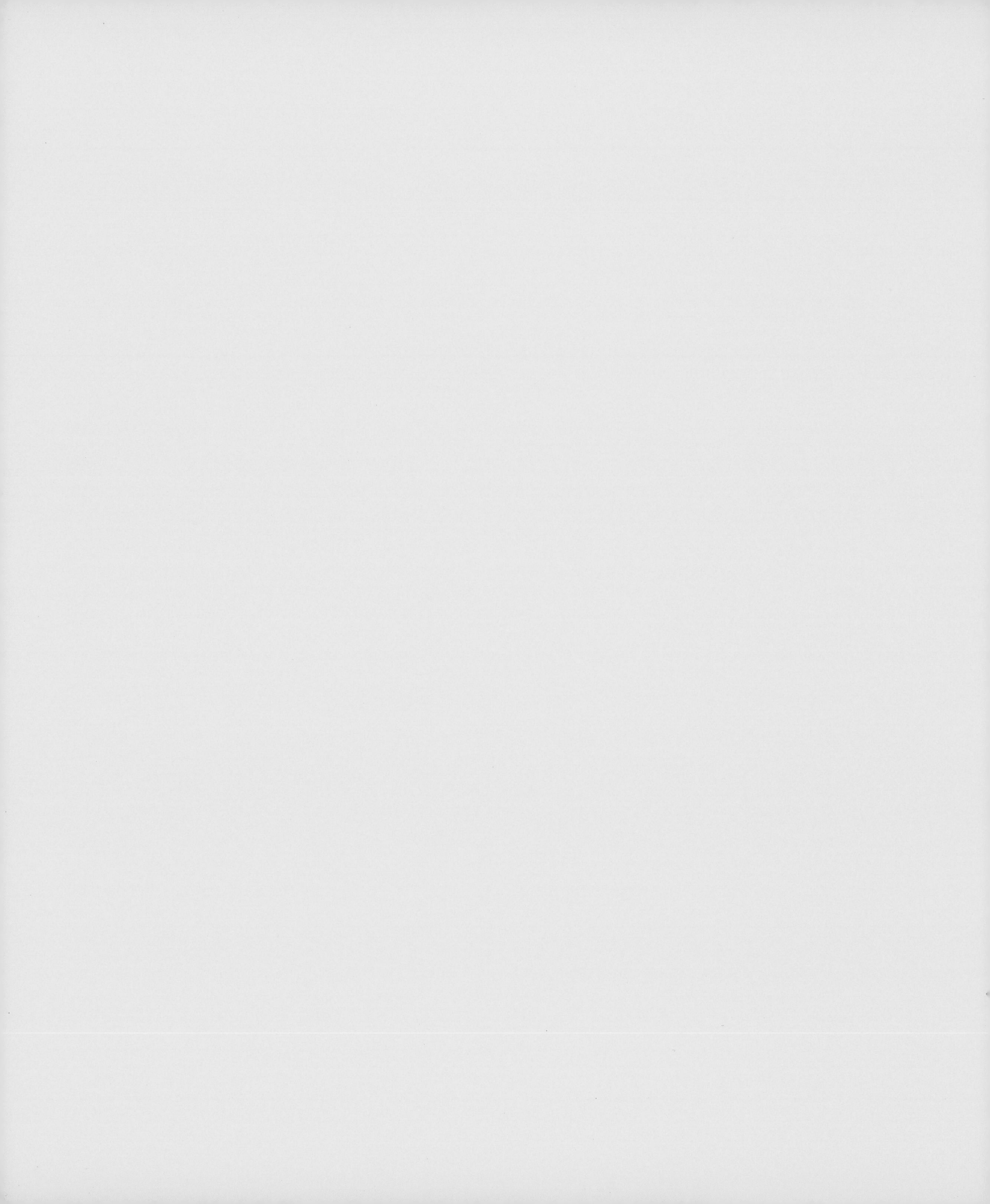